For my brother Peter
with all my love
A.M.

To my dear mother
J.N.

First published in the United States 1991 by
Dial Books for Young Readers
A Division of Penguin Books USA Inc.
375 Hudson Street
New York, New York 10014

Published in Great Britain by ABC
Text copyright © 1991 by Angela McAllister
Pictures copyright © 1991 by Jill Newton
Printed and bound in Great Britain
by MacLehose & Partners for Imago
First Edition
E
1 3 5 7 9 10 8 6 4 2

Library of Congress Cataloging in Publication Data

McAllister, Angela
Matepo/by Angela McAllister; pictures by Jill Newton.
p.   cm.
Summary: Through a series of exchanges with the animals he meets
on his walk through the jungle, Matepo the monkey winds up with the
perfect birthday gift for his mother.
ISBN 0-8037-0838-6
[1. Monkeys—Fiction.   2. Jungle animals—Fiction.]   I. Newton,
Jill, 1964–   ill.   II. Title.
PZ7.M11714Mat1991 [E]—dc20 90-33113 CIP   AC

The full-color artwork was prepared with ink and watercolors.
It was then color-separated and reproduced as red, blue, yellow,
and black halftones.

MATEPO

ANGELA McALLISTER
PICTURES BY JILL NEWTON

Dial Books for Young Readers New York

M1142m

One hot morning Matepo the
monkey climbed up to the
highest treetop to gather fruit
as a present for his mother.
Above the canopy of the jungle
the blue sky was bright with
butterflies and birds of paradise.
There the fruit was
swollen with

juice and ripe with the sun. Matepo gathered honey
pears, fire-fruit, sweet nanas, plump yamas, and
fragrant juleberries, as much as he could carry,
and carefully climbed down to the steamy
swamp below.

But as he stepped into the shadows, a coiled root at his feet suddenly twisted and heaved. Poor Matepo was thrown to the ground, and all his precious fruit tumbled into the muddy swamp. The twisting root uncoiled into Ssur the anaconda who was very sorry to see what had happened.

"Let us not get upset
about fruit," said Matepo wisely.
"But what am I to give my mother now?"
Ssur slithered off into the undergrowth and
quickly returned with a necklace of pearly shells.
"Maybe your mother would like thisss," he offered.
"Its lassst owner was an essspecially plump piglet.
Please take it, I insissst."
And with a ripple and a rustle he was gone.

Matepo knew his mother
really wanted fruit, but he put on the
necklace and started for home. Before long
he heard an echoing screech, and Pati-pol-pol
the parrot swooped down on her brilliant wings.
"Pretty necklace, pretty necklace!" she cried.
"Pretty Pati, pretty Pati!"

Why should I keep the necklace if I have no use for it? thought Matepo. So he gave it to Pati-pol-pol and it suited her well. In return she gave Matepo two fabulous tail feathers that shimmered with blues and greens of the sea and pinks and purples of the sunset. Then up she soared, to be admired among the birds of paradise.

Matepo knew his mother really wanted fruit, but he tucked the feathers behind his ears and started for home. As he swung on the creepers in the trees, Matepo noticed Quilla the porcupine sobbing at the water's edge below. "What makes you so sad?" he asked as he landed gently beside her.

"My children have wandered away from home,"
cried Quilla, "and I hear them call me beyond
the water but I cannot get across."

Just then the swamp waters swelled and the glassy, green eyes of Emeraldo the alligator broke the surface. "Who is crying salt tears into my swamp?" he asked in a slow, deep voice.

"We need your help, Emeraldo," said Matepo. "Will you carry Quilla across the water to her children?"

Emeraldo blinked thoughtfully. "If you will give me those beautiful feathers, I will take Quilla across the swamp. But she must be careful, for those spines are long and sharp."

Matepo agreed, but he was curious to know why the alligator wanted Pati-pol-pol's feathers.

"All day long I lie low in this cool, dark swamp, watching the birds of the air fly free," Emeraldo explained. "Those feathers have soared high above the canopy of the jungle and that is why they please me so."

Then, with Matepo on his back holding Pati-pol-pol's feathers, Emeraldo glided across the water.

At the far bank Emeraldo took
Pati-pol-pol's feathers and, smiling,
slithered silently away into the shadows.

Quilla found her lost children and was very
grateful to Matepo. "Please accept this bristle brush
of our finest spines," she said. "It will not replace
your feathers, but perhaps it will be useful."

Matepo knew his mother really wanted
fruit, but not wishing to offend Quilla, he took
the bristle brush and continued on his way. When
he was almost home, Matepo heard a strange
commotion coming from a clearing nearby. As he crept
close, he saw Oro the orangutan wriggling and scratching
in a great cloud of dust.

"Ants! Ants!" bellowed Oro when he saw Matepo.

In an instant Matepo took the bristle brush and began combing Oro's long hair which was crawling with ants. When every last ant was gone, Oro sat on the grass and laughed loud and long. "I must have gone to sleep on an anthill," he explained to Matepo. "I thought I would never stop scratching!"

"I think you need this bristle brush more than I do," offered Matepo.

Oro was very grateful. "But what can I give you in return?" he said. "I only have fruit — "

Matepo's eyes lit up. "Fruit would be perfect!" he said.

So Oro brought honey pears, fire-fruit, sweet nanas, plump yamas, and fragrant juleberries, as much as Matepo could carry, in exchange for the bristle brush. Then, keeping out of the shadows, with careful steps, Matepo went home.

When his mother saw the luscious fruits, she gasped with delight. "How did you know that was just what I really wanted?" she asked her son happily.

But she heard no reply, for Matepo had already
gone off again to play in the fabulous jungle.

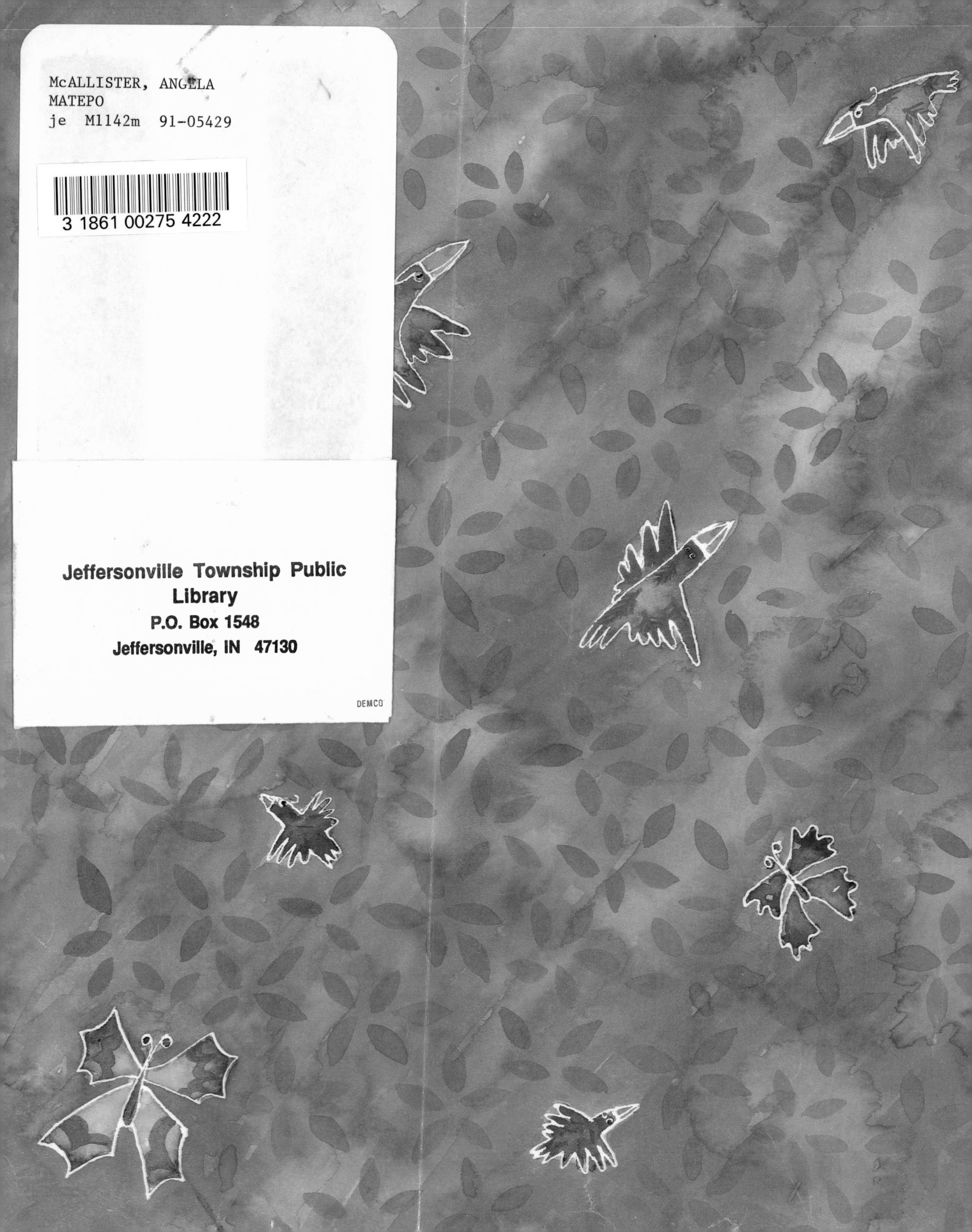